By Rosa Nam, M.Ed.
Illustrated by Chris Chalik

Publishing Credits

Rachelle Cracchiolo, M.S.Ed., *Publisher*
Conni Medina, M.A.Ed., *Editor in Chief*
Nika Fabienke, Ed.D., *Content Director*
Véronique Bos, *Creative Director*
Shaun N. Bernadou, *Art Director*
Noelle Cristea, M.A.Ed., *Senior Editor*
John Leach, *Assistant Editor*
Jess Johnson, *Graphic Designer*

Image Credits

Illustrated by Chris Chalik

Library of Congress Cataloging-in-Publication Data

Names: Nam, Rosa, author. | Chalik, Chris, illustrator.
Title: Robot rescue / by Rosa Nam M.Ed. ; illustrated by Chris Chalik.
Description: Huntington Beach, CA : Teacher Created Materials, [2020] |
  Includes book club questions. | Audience: Age 13. | Audience: Grades
  4-6.
Identifiers: LCCN 2019031479 (print) | LCCN 2019031480 (ebook) | ISBN
  9781644913628 (paperback) | ISBN 9781644914526 (ebook)
Subjects: LCSH: Readers (Elementary) | Robots--Juvenile fiction. | Outer
  space--Exploration--Juvenile fiction.
Classification: LCC PE1119 .N277 2020 (print) | LCC PE1119 (ebook) | DDC
  428.6/2--dc23
LC record available at https://lccn.loc.gov/2019031479
LC ebook record available at https://lccn.loc.gov/2019031480

TCM Teacher Created Materials

5301 Oceanus Drive
Huntington Beach, CA 92649-1030
www.tcmpub.com

ISBN 978-1-6449-1362-8

© 2020 Teacher Created Materials, Inc.
Printed in China
Nordica.082019.CA21901551

Table of Contents

CHAPTER ONE

It's Alive

Fifty kilometers away from mission control, Roy's engine hummed quietly. He continued on his usual path toward the object in the distance. He made his way across the windy desert, navigating boulders, craters, and empty riverbeds. On the clock, it was early morning, but you could never tell, since it didn't get dark on this side of the planet. Roy was a robot. He looked like an oversize cat, minus all the fur, with wheels and extra arms. He could move on all fours or use two all-terrain wheels to roll around.

As Roy approached the black blob, he stuck two thin arms out of the right side of his body. He picked up the object to take a good look at the specimen.

"Anna, are you seeing this?"

"Wha—Hello?" said Anna into her wristcom.

"Daydreaming again?" asked Roy.

"No," lied Anna.

Actually, she *had* been daydreaming. She had been fantasizing about being the first teenager awarded the Nobel Prize for "outstanding research in space." She was standing onstage while thousands of people clapped for her. But Roy snapped her back to reality. She was supposed to be observing as he conducted his morning survey.

She had followed her parents and 20 of the brightest minds on Earth to the first colonial outpost in deep space. Well, technically she had been given two options—neither of which was all that great. Either follow her parents or attend a boarding school near her great aunt who perpetually smelled like ginseng. She had settled for space. Watching her creation, Roy, explore was her job this month.

Next month, she would move to the hydroponic hanging gardens. Those were on the side of the cliff where the crew had built their base. But until then, she was cooped up in a stuffy bunker.

Anna clicked on the monitor to see Roy's point of view.

"Another dead bug," said Anna in disappointment. "Nothing new."

It was all the same routine now. Anna had found it exciting the first 10 or so times, but now it was pretty boring. Roy would find a bug, scan it for life, find that it was likely dead, and still bring it back to the lab. The bugs had brown shells as hard as the surface of the planet they lived on. They were either really good at playing dead or they were just dead. Up to this point, it had always been the latter.

Anna had gotten her hopes up once. One bug had appeared to be sleeping; but it had a tiny electrical pulse. Unfortunately, a dust storm had interfered with Roy's instruments. After they had run tests back at the lab, Anna was disappointed to find that the bug was just as dead as the rest.

She had hoped that as the youngest team member—who was really part of the crew because of her parents—she would be able to do something noteworthy. However, all she was really good for was cafeteria duty and staying out of the way of the adults.

"This is different. I detect an electrical pulse," said Roy. He focused the thermal scanner over the bug and

waited for the reading. Anna rested her face in her hands and watched Roy, expecting another failure. The screen turned from black to red, and then on the monitor, a long bug with six legs appeared. It wiggled.

Anna bolted upright in her chair. "Do you see that?" she asked.

"Affirmative." Roy carefully tucked the specimen into a bag and dropped it into his storage compartment.

"This is incredible! Look around for others!" Anna waited for a response but only heard static. The monitor suddenly turned hazy like swimming in murky water, and all she could make out were dull rays of light. The effect was disorienting. The speaker screeched suddenly, and Anna turned down the volume.

"Anna, I—" Roy never completed his statement as a large boulder crashed into him with enough force to make Anna jump back from the screen. The camera went pitch black.

CHAPTER TWO

Calling for Backup

Anna scrolled through Roy's cameras, but the feeds were empty. She checked Roy's GPS locator to find his coordinates but only got an error message. She started to panic. What if something terrible had happened to Roy? He was her only friend—even if she had designed and built him—on this side of the galaxy. Anna paused and began to take in deep breaths like she had learned in astronaut training.

She dialed Alfie, the resident robot in the space station orbiting the planet. Alfie could see the entire planet through a massive satellite and was the go-to person, or robot, when anything went wrong. He could help locate Roy. Alfie had been built by Anna's parents and was the first new-age robot ever created. He was tall with two legs, a boxy head, and six arms.

"Ahoy, Anna!" he cried in his pirate accent. (That was Anna's father's *personality* programming.)

"Alfie, Roy's in trouble! I need everything you can give me on his location."

"Oy! Cat get lost? Just teasing. Checking now."

Alfie typed rapidly with his many arms and scanned the satellite images across his monitors.

He zoomed into the planet's surface

with the orbital telescope. Once
he found Roy, Alfie transmitted his
location to Anna.

"Coming your way." This time, he
spoke in a Scottish accent.

She waited impatiently as the data
transferred to her wristcom. *Hurry up.*

"What's the plan?" asked Alfie.

"I'm calling Dr. Flores as soon as
we're done," said Anna, "and we're
going to rescue him."

Honestly, she wished she didn't have
to rely on adults all the time, but now
was not the time to break the rules.
The download finished.

"Anna to the rescue! I'll be watching
out for you. Be careful, lassie."

"Will do." Anna thanked Alfie,
grabbed her bag, and dialed Dr. Flores,
the defense coordinator.

Anna packed the last of their
provisions into the cross-planet rover,
also known as the C-PR. Hopefully,
they would only be gone for a few
hours, but it was protocol to be

overprepared. Dr. Flores ran around the rover checking and re-checking for damage. The crew had a total of three C-PRs: one that was larger and meant for multi-day excursions and two smaller ones for single-day trips. The day-trip C-PRs were designated for a driver and a passenger, with a small galley and an emergency sleeping compartment in the back. They were taking one of the smaller ones to rescue Roy.

CHAPTER THREE

Rescue Mission

Anna stood in the doorway of the C-PR, anxiously checking her watch.

"Dr. Flores?" Twenty minutes had already passed since she had lost contact with Roy.

"Almost done." After two more laps around the C-PR, Dr. Flores was finished with her thorough inspection.

The two took their seats and buckled in.

The C-PR's pneumatic door hissed shut. The bay doors of the facility opened, spilling light into the docking station. Soon, they were off, trailing dust behind as they made their way across the red desert.

"We should be there within the hour," said Dr. Flores, who noticed that

Anna was bouncing her leg and tapping on the armrest.

"Roy will be okay," reassured Dr. Flores. Anna smiled half-heartedly.

After that, a silence fell between them, and they both gazed out the windshield. The landscape sometimes reminded Anna of Mars, but with more cliffs and canyons. Rather than taking

the path of least resistance, Dr. Flores drove straight over boulders and through craters to get to Roy as quickly as possible. The shock absorbers in the C-PR were first-class, but it was still a bumpy ride.

When the landscape finally smoothed out, Dr. Flores switched the C-PR to autopilot and went back to the galley to grab snacks. Anna stared through the windshield, watching the barren landscape pass by. There was literally nothing to see, no matter where she looked. The ground was dry and parched from lack of rain.

The crew had been living on the planet for over 80 days, and it had not rained once, not a single drop—though it looked like storm clouds were forming. Anna got excited for a second, but then she thought about Roy and what he might be doing at that moment. What if he was severely injured? Most of the equipment she had used to build Roy she had brought from Earth, and it's not like the base had extra solar cells lying around. What if they didn't have any vital spare parts on the base? She had spent over 200 hours working on her new-age robot and was rather invested in Roy's welfare. But beyond that, he was her best friend and irreplaceable.

Anna's wristcom vibrated, notifying her that Alfie was calling.

"Anna, I hope you're surviving the turbulence. I've heard stories about Dr. Flores's driving."

"Har, har. Very funny," said Dr. Flores sarcastically.

Alfie chuckled. "I wanted you two to know that the storm down there is growing, and it looks like it's headed straight your way. Blimey, it's a big one!"

"Copy that," said Dr. Flores, who returned to her seat carrying two sandwiches and two bottles of water. She passed a set to Anna, who thanked her.

"Let's see whether we can speed things up, shall we?" Dr. Flores took a huge bite of her sandwich and pressed on the accelerator.

Soon they were swallowed up by the dusty darkness. Sand pelted the sides of the C-PR making it sound as though it were raining. The sand became so dense that the headlights couldn't penetrate it. Instead, the light bounced off the sand and back into the rover, so Dr. Flores turned them off and switched on the fog lights. She navigated using a combination of satellite imagery and radar, since the sand was blinding them. After 10 minutes or so—though it seemed much longer in the turbulence—the radar picked up Roy's signal.

"I see him!" called Anna with relief.

Dr. Flores maneuvered the C-PR and made a beeline straight toward Roy.

CHAPTER FOUR

Sandstorm

The signal strengthened as they approached Roy, but so did the storm. The small sand pellets grew to the size of beads and occasionally clumped together and popped against the C-PR. It sounded like a hailstorm. One especially large rock smacked straight into the windshield. Luckily, it bounced off without cracking the glass.

"That was close," said Dr. Flores with a gasp.

"That really was," said Anna, but she had spoken too soon. A piece of debris burst straight through the windshield, right in front of Dr. Flores's head.

"Ahh!" She ducked just in time but jerked the steering wheel, driving the C-PR headfirst into a shallow crater. Sand began dumping through the hole and onto the front consoles as Dr. Flores and Anna struggled to unbuckle their seatbelts.

Dr. Flores was the first to free herself and rushed to the back of the rover for the emergency tools. Anna finally managed to unbuckle herself and fell backward. Dr. Flores grabbed a device that looked like a handheld extinguisher and ordered Anna to get back. She removed the emergency clip from the trigger and pointed the nozzle at the hole. Foam spread out against the windshield like a spiderweb. It

closed the hole for a second, but the
pressure was too strong and the sand
rushed back in.

Dr. Flores abandoned the device
and pressed her hands against the
windshield, using them as a plug. "We
need something to block the flow,"
she shouted.

Anna looked around desperately for

something, anything, that would work. She saw her backpack and immediately had an idea. She reached into it and grabbed her handy roll of super sticky tape. Anna tossed it to Dr. Flores, who began tearing strips of tape with her teeth and sticking them across the glass.

As soon as the sand ebbed, Dr. Flores grabbed the extinguisher and pulled the trigger again. The nozzle spewed fluffy foam onto the glass. It congealed, hardened, and then changed colors to be completely transparent, sealing the windshield. Only the gray strips of tape remained visible.

Dr. Flores pulled Anna into a big hug. "You, my young friend, just saved our lives." Anna relaxed into the hug and sighed in relief.

"Now let's get out of here," said Dr. Flores. The two climbed back into their seats, and Dr. Flores engaged the thrusters and drove the C-PR up and out of the crater.

CHAPTER FIVE

Falling into Place

Dr. Flores parked the C-PR safely above ground and away from the crater. She checked the radar and was surprised to see that it showed that Roy's location aligned exactly with their position. Anna looked around the inside of the C-PR puzzled, even though she knew that there was no way

Roy could be there. The two looked back at the radar and heard a loud bang. The sound came from on top of the C-PR. They both looked up as an object slid down the windshield like in one of those cartoons—but this was real life. The dark body continued sliding long enough for them to get a good look through the strips of tape. It was Roy.

He opened one eye, waved hello, and slipped out of sight. They could see that he was missing an arm.

Dr. Flores ran to the back of the C-PR, slipped on her hazard suit, and with a quick thumbs-up to Anna, exited through the airlock chamber. Anna paced back and forth across the sandy floor, waiting in anticipation. She heard

scraping and a few bumps against the rover before the door hissed open and she saw Dr. Flores, covered with flecks of sand, step back inside holding a mangled-looking Roy in her arms.

Anna ran over to Roy and unleashed a torrent of questions, to which Roy simply responded, "Hi. Rain," and went right into sleep mode.

"Okay…" replied Anna.

She examined Roy closely, confused about his last remark and worried that he had hit his head. The energy panel on his chest read "dangerously low battery," and a few plates of armor had been badly damaged.

In addition to his missing arm, one wheel was completely missing. But he could be refurbished. Anna placed Roy in a cargo net so he would be safe on the journey back to the base. The storm was even stronger now and jostling the C-PR.

"The wind is really picking up," said Anna.

"It's not wind," said Dr. Flores slowly. "It's rain."

The two marveled, open-mouthed at the sight of rain. They were engulfed in a torrential downpour as the rain came sideways. It soaked the dry ground and caused little rivers to form, snaking their way across the land like veins. Dr. Flores drove a bit slower and more carefully this time. They made it back to the base in time for dinner, excited to talk to the others about the spectacular change in weather.

The entire base was buzzing with talk of the rain. A few scientists had even mentioned something about possibly seeing live bugs in the garden. However, when they took a closer look, the bugs had disappeared. Anna wondered whether the rain had anything to do with the live bug they found.

The next week, Roy was as good as new. Even better, he had managed to secure the specimen from the week before. It had been safe within his hull compartment. It was now being looked at by the resident biologist.

Anna and Roy arrived at the laboratory after lunch and watched the insect crawl around the enclosed glass tank. It was most definitely alive.

"What you two found is amazing," said the biologist. "This is remarkable. This is going to change everything."

Anna beamed with pride. Not only had she successfully rescued Roy with Dr. Flores's help, but she and Roy had also discovered the first live specimen on the planet. Who knew what else they would find and how it could contribute to science? For the first time since arriving on the planet, Anna felt like part of the team. And who knew? Maybe that Nobel Prize would actually become a reality someday.

About Us

The Author
Rosa Nam taught high school English for a number of years. Now, she teaches future teachers. Although her first choice for reading is literary fiction, science fiction and stories about space travel hold a special place in her heart. She is excited for future space travel to distant planets like Mars and reading more stories about exploring galaxies near and far.

The Illustrator
Chris Chalik lives and works in London. In his work, he likes to create a dark, mysterious mood. He has co-authored a graphic novel and won awards for his comic work. He is originally from Poland.